DUCK!

meg mcKinlay

illustrated by

Nathaniel Eckstrom

CANDLEWICK PRESS

It was a quiet afternoon on the farm. The horse was swishing his tail, and the cow was chewing her cud. The pig was wallowing in the mud, and the sheep was sheeping on the grass.

It was a quiet afternoon on the farm, when suddenly . . .

"Duck?" The horse snorted. "No, no! You're mistaken, my friend. *You* are a duck. *I* am a horse. You see — you are small and waddly, and I am noble and tall. I look nothing at all like a —"

"Duck?" The cow frowned. "Don't be ridiculous! *You* are a duck, and *he* is a horse, and *I* am a cow. You see — you have funny webbed feet, and I have these fine cloven hooves. I have no idea why you would call me a —"

"Duck?" The pig squealed.
"Please! *You* are a duck, and *he* is a horse,
and *she* is a cow, and *I* am a pig. You see —
you have a poky little beak, and I have a
fine pink snout. Why on earth would
you think I am a —"

"Duck?" The sheep scoffed. "Are you even listening? *You* are a duck, and *he* is a horse, and *she* is a cow, and *he* is a pig, and *I* am a sheep. You see — you have fluffy little feathers, and I have a fine woolly coat. I have absolutely nothing in common with a—"

"Now **listen.**
You need to stop this nonsense
right **now.**"

"You have to understand
that everyone is different."

"In fact, most are **not.**"

"That's just how the world is."

"Imagine how **boring** it would be if everyone were a duck."

"BUT —"

"Stop! Not one more word!"

"You are the **rudest** duck we've ever met."

"You can't just run around shouting . . ."

"You can't just run around yelling your **name**."

"Oh, you're right.
Quite right.
I do apologize.
I should never have said DUCK.

I should have said . . ."

For all the little folk who have
important things to say

M. M.

For Brigham

N. E.

Text copyright © 2018 by Meg McKinlay
Illustrations copyright © 2018 by Nathaniel Eckstrom

First U.S. edition 2019
First published by Walker Books Australia 2018

Library of Congress Catalog Card Number pending
ISBN 978-1-5362-0422-3

19 20 21 22 23 24 LEO 10 9 8 7 6 5 4 3 2 1

Printed in Heshan, Guangdong, China

This book was typeset in Historical.
The illustrations were done in pencil, acrylic, and digital art.

Candlewick Press
99 Dover Street
Somerville, Massachusetts 02144

visit us at www.candlewick.com

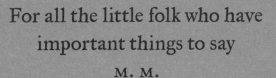